AMELIA EARHART:
MISSING, DECLARED DEAD

by

Anita Larsen

Illustrated by
Marcy Ramsey

CRESTWOOD HOUSE
NEW YORK

Maxwell Macmillan Canada
Toronto

Maxwell Macmillan International
New York   Oxford   Singapore   Sydney

Library of Congress Cataloging-in-Publication Data
Larsen, Anita.

Amelia Earhart: missing, declared dead / by Anita Larsen. — 1st ed.
p. cm. — (History's mysteries)
Includes bibliographical references and index.
Summary: Reviews the haunting case of Amelia Earhart's disappearance in 1937 while attempting an around-the-world flight and offers possible scenarios of what might actually have happened.
ISBN 0-89686-613-0
1. Earhart, Amelia, 1897–1937—Juvenile literature. 2. Air pilots—United States—Biography—Juvenile literature. [1. Earhart, Amelia, 1897–1937. 2. Missing persons. 3. Air pilots.] I. Title.
II. Series.
TL540.E3L37 1992
629.13'092—dc20
[B]   91-19246
                                                                                  CIP
                                                                                   AC

Copyright © 1992 Crestwood House, Macmillan Publishing Company

Crestwood House
Macmillan Publishing Company
866 Third Avenue
New York, NY 10022

Maxwell Macmillan Canada, Inc.
1200 Eglinton Avenue East
Suite 200
Don Mills, Ontario M3C 3N1

Macmillan Publishing Company is part of the Maxwell Communication Group of Companies.

First edition

Printed in the United States of America

10 9 8 7 6 5 4 3 2 1

CONTENTS

THE CASE OPENS
▲▲▲▲▲▲▲▲▲▲▲▲▲▲▲▲▲▲▲▲▲▲▲▲▲▲▲▲▲▲

It is midmorning, July 2, 1937.

World-famous pilot Amelia Earhart and her navigator, Fred Noonan, are in the small cockpit of their specially equipped, twin-engine Lockheed Electra.

Today, Earhart and Noonan plan to fly 2,556 miles, from Lae, New Guinea, to Howland Island, a tiny spot in the vast Pacific Ocean. The flight is one leg of an around-the-world adventure that began almost four months before on March 17. Earhart is flying around the earth at its widest point—the equator. She is traveling from west to east.

Her original plan had been to fly around the world from east to west. She planned to begin in Oakland and fly to Hawaii. From there she would fly south to Howland Island, then to Australia, Arabia, Africa and Brazil before returning to

California. The trip from Oakland to Hawaii went well. But on takeoff from Hawaii to Howland, the Electra veered to the right on the runway. When Earhart tried to correct the plane, it turned sharply. The landing gear collapsed and a wing was damaged. Gasoline poured from the wing tanks. Earhart coolly cut the engines, knowing that just one spark could turn the plane into a fireball. She later wrote she thought, "If we don't burn up, I want to try again."

Repairs would take two months. Earhart returned to California to replan her route. The delay meant that global weather patterns would change. Earhart rescheduled her trip to fly from west to east. She would set out from Miami, Florida, on June 1 this time. This added 2,000 miles to her trip. It left the hazardous leg from Howland to Hawaii until the end.

Now they sit on the runway in Lae, New Guinea, waiting to take off for Howland Island. On advice from the Guinea Airways radio operator, Earhart has changed today's flight plan. Her new route will lead to Nukumanu Island, 750 miles east of Lae. Using other islands as landmarks, Earhart will reach Nukumanu just before sunset. Then she will turn northeast to fly over Naurau Island in the night. Lights will be left on to guide her.

When she passes Naurau, Earhart will be a little over halfway to Howland. During the long night, she will fly over the British-held Gilbert Islands. Noonan will navigate by the stars.

But night is still a long way away as the Electra taxis down the 3,500-foot-long Lae runway. It has been hacked out of the jungle and ends up with a sheer drop to the sea. The fuel-heavy plane must first lift off. Because of the weight, that is difficult.

The plane lumbers down the runway under the glaring sun. Finally, only 50 yards from the end, the Electra lifts off.

Fred Noonan is worried. His chronometers, or clocks, haven't been set properly. They are essential for navigating by the stars. If they're off by one minute, there will be an error of four miles in his estimate of where they are. If Earhart is off one degree on the compass, she will be one mile off course for every sixty air miles covered. To find tiny Howland, the fliers can make few mistakes.

At 5:20 P.M. Earhart radios back to Lae. The plane is 759 miles out. It is on course, and the weather is clear. Earhart expects to be nearing Howland by dawn. She will get there by homing in on radio signals sent by the *Itasca*.

By midnight, the *Itasca's* searchlights sweep the sky, a beacon for the incoming plane. The cutter's boilers are stoked and ready to give off clouds of smoke to guide the plane if it arrives during the day. The Electra and the small ship also have direction finders on board. A third direction finder has been installed at Howland. This one is an experimental model loaned by the navy.

There are limits to what the direction finders can do. They can use only certain frequencies. The signals must be strong, and they must last at least two minutes so the operator can pinpoint the locations.

At midnight, the *Itasca* begins transmitting voice and telegraph messages. The first message from Earhart comes at 2:45 A.M. Her voice is calm. "Cloudy and overcast," she says. The rest of the message is lost in static.

At 3:00 A.M. the *Itasca* sends the weather report. It is clear and the wind is coming from the east at eight miles per hour. Then the ship begins a telegraph transmission of the letter "A" in Morse code. A short beep followed by a long beat is repeated over and over. This signal will guide the Electra to Howland.

At 3:30, the *Itasca* sends another weather report

and asks Earhart to report her position when she next broadcasts. They ask her what time she expects to arrive.

At 3:45 Earhart sends a voice message reporting overcast conditions. A little before 5 A.M. her voice is heard again. The transmission is poor. No one can understand her.

Her next call comes at 6:15. She's "about two hundred miles out" and can see no land. She asks the *Itasca* to take a bearing on her. She whistles into her microphone to help the direction finder work. But her whistle produces only static. Her next whistle comes half an hour later. But Earhart is on the air too briefly for the direction finder to work.

At 7:42, Earhart's voice breaks clearly into the radio room: "We must be on you, but cannot see you. But gas is running low. Been unable to reach you by radio. We are flying at altitude 1,000 feet."

The radio men in the *Itasca* think Earhart can't be far away because her signal is so strong. She calls again at 7:58. Her voice is loud and clear. She and Noonan are circling. The *Itasca* immediately sends out a long series of Morse code letter As.

At 8:45 Earhart is heard clearly. "We are on line of position 157 dash 337. Will repeat this message on 6210 kilocycles. Wait, listening on 6210 kilocycles. We are running north and south."

This is her last transmission. No one is quite sure what she means by "line of position." It does not help them pinpoint her position. The *Itasca* crew waits. Earhart probably has fuel to last until 10 A.M.

Within hours after 10 A.M. the largest sea search in the history of the U.S. Navy is ordered by President Franklin Roosevelt. The search lasts 17 days, until July 19. Then it is called off. No trace of Earhart, Noonan or the Electra has been found. The official report is: "Lost at sea."

THE CASE FILE

▲▲▲▲▲▲▲▲▲▲▲▲▲▲▲▲▲▲▲▲▲▲▲▲▲▲▲▲▲

A GENTLE REBEL

Amelia Earhart loved adventure and excitement all her life. The brave pilot who disappeared on that July day in 1937 was always a rebel with a strong spirit and great determination.

Amelia was born on July 24, 1897. At that time girls wore long skirts and played with dolls. But Amelia's parents allowed her to be herself. If she and her sister, Muriel, wanted footballs for Christmas, they got them.

Her father, Edwin, was a claims agent for railroad companies. If freight was damaged in shipment, Edwin dealt with the shippers. He was paid a fee for each claim he settled instead of earning a salary. His work often took him away from home. He usually took his wife with him. So the girls spent the school year with their grandparents. During the summer they stayed with their parents.

In 1907 Edwin Earhart was promoted to a salaried railroad job. That meant the family had to move. In 1908 the girls went to live full-time with their parents in Des Moines, Iowa.

On Amelia's birthday that year, Edwin took the family to the Iowa State Fair. A newfangled invention was supposed to be there—an airplane. He wanted to see it. A lady watching as the plane took off told Amelia, "Look, dear, it flies!" Amelia was more interested in the funny 17-cent hat she'd just bought.

While living in Des Moines, a serious family problem developed: Amelia's father became an alcoholic. He lost job after job. The family moved often. Finally, the Earharts separated. The girls and their mother moved to Chicago when Amelia was in high school.

"THE GIRL IN BROWN, WHO WALKS ALONE"

In Chicago, Amelia was a loner. The slogan under her picture in the senior yearbook read, "The girl in brown, who walks alone." It hurt.

In 1917 Amelia attended a school near Philadelphia. During Christmas she went to Toronto to visit Muriel, who was in school there.

Canada had already been in World War I for three years. Amelia volunteered as a nurse's aide in a

veterans' hospital. She worked there ten hours a day until the war ended late in 1918. For the first time, Amelia realized how much pain and injury war meant.

Sometimes Amelia, Muriel and their friends were invited to watch the flights made by officers from the nearby Canadian Flying School. One day Amelia saw a little red plane. It was the first time she really knew what she wanted to do. She wanted to fly.

But Amelia had to wait to fulfill that dream. She went to New York City and entered Barnard College of Columbia University. She began to study medicine. This was cut short when her parents, who had reunited, asked Amelia to come to Los Angeles and live with them. Thinking that she could help her parents avoid divorce, Amelia went.

In California, she discovered air circuses. These were entertainments put on by wartime fliers. They were trying to make a living after the war doing stunt flying. Edwin arranged a trial flight for Amelia with one of the pilots. After one flight, she was hooked.

Amelia took flying lessons from Neta Snook, one of the first women pilots in America. In 1921 she made her first solo flight. By the next summer, she owned her own plane. It was a secondhand, yellow Kiner Canary that had been built locally.

By the summer of 1924, the Earharts had decided to divorce. Amelia sold her plane and bought a bright yellow car. She and her mother drove to Boston where Muriel was now teaching. Amelia found a job there as a social worker at Denison House, a settlement house for Boston's underprivileged. She would remain there for the next several years.

THE FIRST WOMAN TO FLY THE ATLANTIC

In 1927 Charles Lindbergh flew the first solo flight across the Atlantic Ocean. This feat earned him the nickname Lucky Lindy. It made him a world hero.

Lindbergh's historic flight inspired Amy Phipps Guest, a wealthy American living in England, to buy a plane. She named the plane *Friendship*. Guest wanted to fly across the Atlantic also, but her family thought it was too dangerous. Guest was determined to find an American woman pilot to take her place.

Guest's search led her to George Palmer Putnam,

a book publisher in New York City. Putnam had promoted several adventures in the past. He came up with a number of names. One of them was Amelia Earhart.

Earhart sounded perfect. By this time she had owned two planes. Guest's selection committee interviewed Earhart in New York and decided she *was* perfect.

Earhart didn't hesitate when told she'd been chosen for the flight. She would be a passenger, but she would also be captain and make all the decisions. Besides Amelia, the crew consisted of Wilmer Stutz, pilot, and Louis Gordon, mechanic. Amelia hoped she would have a chance to pilot the plane part of the way herself.

Preparations for the flight were secret. No one, not even Earhart's family, knew she would be on it. Before she left, she wrote what she called "popping off letters," or farewell letters, to each of her parents. The one to her father began, "Hooray for the grand adventure! I wish I had won, but it was worthwhile anyway."

Conditions were right for takeoff late on the morning of June 17, 1928. Even then, the plane had to taxi down the runway four times before it could get enough wind lift.

Back then, pilots often plotted their flight courses using road maps or landmarks on the ground. But there were no maps or landmarks on the ocean. *Friendship,* which flew out of Newfoundland, was headed for Ireland, but it got lost. The plane landed in the harbor outside Burry Port, Wales.

No one onshore seemed excited about the landing. But soon the *Friendship* crew was brought ashore and the news about who they were got out. Thousands of Welsh turned out to greet them. The next day Earhart and her mates met Mrs. Guest, the press and crowds of wellwishers.

The flight brought Earhart fame. She was happy about this, but thought Stutz and Gordon deserved the credit for having actually flown the *Friendship.*

The publicity also brought her two nicknames. One was Lady Lindy, which irritated her. To keep her self-respect, Earhart vowed that someday she would fly the Atlantic solo. The other nickname was better—AE. That one started when she and George Putnam exchanged telegrams, each signing with initials.

When she was back in America, Putnam suggested that Earhart live with him and his wife in Rye, New York, so she could write a book about the flight. He published Amelia's book, *20 Hrs., 40*

Min., and managed the many requests for magazine articles and speeches by Earhart.

Earhart's life soon revolved around writing, lecturing and flying. In 1928 she became the first woman to fly from the Atlantic to the Pacific coasts and back again. Earhart had not intentionally set out to do that. She had just wanted to be in the air.

The year 1930 was an eventful one for Earhart. Her father died, and she paid all his debts. She also helped start a new venture for the times—a passenger airline. She set flight speed records for women. She learned to fly an autogiro, an early helicopter. She even set records in that.

Also in 1930, Earhart accepted the sixth of Putnam's marriage proposals. He was divorced now, and Earhart had decided she could trust him not to trap her in a conventional marriage. They were married on February 7, 1931. Putnam left publishing, took a job with Paramount Pictures and began to manage Earhart's career.

By spring 1932, Earhart had decided to make good on her private promise after the *Friendship* flight. It was time to fly across the Atlantic alone.

ATLANTIC SOLO

By May, Earhart and her single-engine Lockheed

Vega were ready. On May 19 she heard good weather reports. She didn't even bother to pack. She left for the airport with her leather flying suit, a thermos of soup and some cans of tomato juice.

At 7:12 P.M. on May 20, Earhart took off from Newfoundland. She wanted to land in Paris on the fifth anniversary of Lindbergh's arrival there. It was a fine flight—for the first hours. Then things started to go wrong.

First the altimeter failed. This instrument tells pilots how far above the earth's surface they are. Without either altimeter or clear weather, a pilot could fly straight into the ocean. The weather was fair, so Earhart decided to fly on.

Then the weather turned bad. The moon disappeared behind clouds. A storm blew up. Winds and air pockets tossed the plane and rain pounded it. Lightning flashed in the surrounding clouds. Earhart had to fight with all her strength to stay on course.

About an hour later the weather calmed. But the sky was still cloudy. Earhart caught a glimpse of the moon and decided to fly above the clouds. She climbed, but the plane grew sluggish and slow. It was gathering ice on the wings.

Earhart descended, hoping the warmer weather

below would melt the ice. When she saw waves breaking on the ocean's surface, she leveled off. Then she ran into fog. She headed up again, hoping to find a safe altitude.

But at higher altitudes she found more clouds and fog—and something else alarming. A joining weld on a metal engine part had started to burn through. In time, the crack would widen and spread. The engine part would begin shaking. Continued shaking could affect the whole engine. But she had no choice. She flew on.

At daybreak, Earhart was flying between two layers of clouds. She headed up toward the sun, hoping the ice still clinging to the plane would melt. But the glare forced her down even though she was wearing dark glasses.

By now, the engine part was shaking badly. When Earhart turned on the reserve fuel tanks, she found they were leaking. Reaching Paris was now out of the question. Earhart had to land at the closest possible site.

She landed on a meadow outside Londonderry, Ireland. She had not gotten to Paris, but she had done what she wanted. She had flown the Atlantic solo, and she'd done it in 15 hours and 56 minutes.

The whirlwind of luncheons, ceremonies and

receptions that had marked the end of the *Friendship* flight happened all over again. Earhart's husband came by ship to join her, and they met the royalty of Europe. After the excitement died down, Earhart wrote *The Fun of It.* And still she went on flying and setting records.

One result of her flight was that Earhart and her husband became friends with the new president, Franklin D. Roosevelt, and his wife, Eleanor.

WAR AND RUMORS OF WAR

There was not a lot for people to laugh about in 1933. This was the time of the Great Depression. The U.S. stock market crash of 1929 had shaken the political foundations of nations worldwide.

In 1931, Japanese troops marched into Manchuria, grabbed it away from China and then began eyeing the Soviet Union. In 1936 Italy took Ethiopia, and civil war broke out in Spain. In 1938 Germany made Austria a part of Germany and invaded parts of Czechoslovakia. By 1939 Europe was a battleground.

The United States tried to stay out of the European conflict. But staying out proved to be difficult. Roosevelt's advisers told him that Hitler would continue to expand Germany's borders unless he was stopped. In the Far East, Japan was equally intent on expansion.

In 1937, when Earhart began her last flight, many small islands in the Pacific were under the control of the Japanese. Japan had been put in charge of them by the peace conference that followed World War I. The treaty from that conference said that the islands could not be used for military purposes.

But Japan was secretly preparing these islands for war. The Japanese would not allow foreign ships to dock or foreign planes to land on the islands. They considered all foreigners to be spies. Many foreigners were arrested. Some were even killed.

A SPY MISSION?

When Earhart and Noonan disappeared, the United States asked the Japanese for permission to search their islands. They refused, saying they would search the islands themselves. They reported finding no trace of the missing fliers.

President Roosevelt's massive sea search failed to turn up anything either. Rumors began to circulate. Some people said Earhart and Noonan had been on a secret mission for President Roosevelt. Their mission was to take photos of the illegal Japanese military buildup.

Earhart's mother added fuel to this theory. In 1949, long after her daughter's disappearance, she said, "I am convinced she was on some sort of government mission, probably on verbal orders." Spies are often given unwritten orders so a government can avoid being trapped into war.

Those who disagreed with this theory pointed out that Earhart had flown over the Japanese-held islands at night. Back then, no cameras could take photos at night without flashbulbs, and flashes would have given them away.

A feature film, *Flight for Freedom,* made in 1943, gave this theory a new twist. In the film, a famous woman flier agreed to "get lost" over the islands so American pilots could gather information. While searching for her, they could take photographs of Japanese activity on the islands. The flier was told to hide on the island. Then she learned the Japanese knew about the plan. She crashed her plane into the Pacific so the search could take place anyway.

CAPTURED BUT SURVIVED?

Another twist on the spy theory was offered by Joe Klaas. He took part in Operation Earhart, an unofficial investigation of Earhart's fated flight that was undertaken many years later.

In his 1970 book, *Amelia Earhart Lives,* Klaas said that Earhart's last flight followed the film's basic plot. Government officials had given Earhart a new, experimental model Electra. It flew faster and farther than her own model. The Japanese forced the plane down on Hull Island, south of Howland, captured Earhart and Noonan and took them to Japan. They were held there until the end of the war.

According to this theory, Earhart and Noonan were released when America promised not to try the Japanese emperor as a war criminal. Once home, Earhart and Noonan were sworn to secrecy. They took new names and hid somewhere in the United States.

Operation Earhart investigators even found a woman living in New Jersey whom they said was Earhart. The woman, they thought, looked the way an older Earhart would have looked. She was a pilot, and she wore a military medal that, until that time, had been awarded only to Earhart. The woman was angry. When she threatened to sue Klaas's publishers, his book was taken out of circulation.

More support for this theory comes from a

statement Putnam made early in the search. The Electra's radios could not work if the plane crashed in water, he said. Yet after Earhart's disappearance there were radio messages that officials did not investigate.

On July 4, for example, three operators at a navy radio station on Diamond Head Mountain, Oahu Island, Hawaii, heard a voice on radio frequency 3105, Earhart's frequency. It was a man's voice, and his message could not be understood. Then on July 7, according to navy radio operators, a woman's voice said, "Earhart calling. NRU1— NRU1—calling from KHAQQ. On coral southwest of unknown island. Do not know how long we will . . ." The voice faded. Seconds later, it was heard again: "KHAQQ calling. KHAQQ. We are cut a little . . ." The sound faded and the voice was not heard again. KHAQQ were Earhart's call letters.

To add fuel to this theory, Earhart was declared legally dead only 18 months after she vanished. That process usually takes seven years.

CAPTURED AND EXECUTED?

During and after World War II, American servicemen in the Pacific were told to ask natives for news about prisoners. Natives told of seeing two white people—a woman and a man with a bandaged head. Supposedly, their plane had crashed and they were picked up by a Japanese ship. The two were taken away to prison. Most reports said the woman died of disease and the man was executed.

After the war, a number of people investigated these stories. One was Fred Goerner, a CBS radio broadcaster. He wrote *The Search for Amelia Earhart.* Another was Vincent Loomis, a retired air force officer, who wrote *Amelia Earhart: The Final Story.*

The men conducted thousands of interviews. Their reports offer basically the same theory. Earhart and Noonan were blown off course by a storm. Hopelessly lost, Earhart landed in the shallow water around the Japanese-controlled Marshall Islands, far from Howland. Noonan was injured in the landing; Earhart was not. The Japanese arrested both of them.

A Japanese cargo ship arrived to pick up them and their damaged plane. They were taken to Japanese military headquarters on the island of Saipan and held in prison there. One startling finding was that the Japanese had not searched for the downed fliers as they had promised.

Another surprising twist came in Thomas Devine's 1987 book, *Eyewitness: The Amelia Earhart Incident*. Devine said that he and a friend saw Earhart's plane being burned by Americans at Saipan's tightly guarded Aslito Field. Devine was a former army sergeant who had served on Saipan between 1944 and 1945, after the island had been captured by the United States.

Devine said Secretary of the Navy James Forrestal was also there at the time. But, since Forrestal died in 1948, Devine was unable to question him for the book.

Devine thought U.S. officials destroyed the plane in order to suppress American outrage at the treatment of the missing fliers. The government's postwar policy was to heal the wounds of war, even if it meant concealing the fates of Earhart and Noonan.

Proving any of these theories seems to hinge on finding the graves of the missing fliers on Saipan. Those grave sites have never been found.

THE OFFICIAL POSITION

After Earhart and Noonan disappeared, Putnam said, "I have a hunch they are sitting somewhere on a coral island . . . Fred's probably out sitting on a

rock now catching their dinner with those fishing lines they had aboard."

Government officials tried to prove that hunch correct. President Roosevelt ordered all available men, ships and planes into the search. A force of seven navy ships, including the carrier *Lexington* and its planes, covered 250,000 square miles. But by July 19, when a squadron of 76 search planes returned to the *Lexington,* no sign of Earhart, Noonan or the wreckage of the Electra had been spotted. Officials assumed they were lost at sea.

The equipment Earhart and Noonan left behind at the beginning of the flight makes this position more plausible. A wire antenna about 250 feet long had been installed on the Electra to strengthen its radio signals. Earhart hated reeling it in and out. Someone—no one knows who—ordered its removal. Without the antenna, the Electra would be out of touch with homing signals for hours at a time. The fliers also left behind the telegraph key because neither could send or receive Morse code signals.

Minutes after the Electra would have run out of fuel, the *Itasca* steamed to the northwest. The weather around Howland Island was clear, but there were heavy clouds to the north and west. The static on Earhart's transmissions indicated she had

been in stormy weather. Weather also explained her failure to see the cutter's searchlights and smoke columns.

Today, well over 50 years later, search parties still look for traces of Earhart and Noonan. None have been found.

You have just read the known facts about one of HISTORY'S MYSTERIES. To date, there have been no more answers to the mysteries posed in the story. There are possibilities, though. Read on and see which answer seems the most believable to you. How would you solve the case?

SOLUTIONS

▲▲▲▲▲▲▲▲▲▲▲▲▲▲▲▲▲▲▲▲▲▲▲▲▲▲▲▲▲

EXECUTED AS SPIES

Earhart and Noonan were spying for America. They didn't give their positions to the *Itasca* because that would have also told the Japanese where they were.

The Japanese did not search for Earhart and Noonan as they had promised because they knew the missing fliers were in a Japanese prison. The prisoners couldn't be released because they had seen too much.

The reports made by Pacific Island natives to American servicemen of a white couple arrested by the Japanese are true. The details of those reports blurred over time. But there were few white people in the area in 1937. The couple had to be Earhart and Noonan.

Failing to find the graves of the missing fliers does not mean they were not arrested and executed as spies. The Japanese did not have to bury Earhart and Noonan. They could just as easily have dumped their bodies into the Pacific.

LOST AT SEA

The official position that Earhart and Noonan were lost at sea is correct. The government's massive search turned up no trace of them.

When the fliers left their trailing wire antenna and telegraph key behind, they gambled on perfect weather. The static during Earhart's voice messages proves the weather was bad. So does their inability to see the *Itasca's* searchlight and smoke column. The malfunctioning chronometers Noonan was concerned about after the Electra lifted off from Lae, New Guinea, caused another error. The fliers did not turn back to repair the clocks. But the clock's readings were essential for navigating by the stars. Earhart did not give her position to the *Itasca* because she and Noonan simply did not know where they were.

SURVIVED

Earhart and Noonan were American spies. Earhart would certainly have helped President Roosevelt. After all, adventure appealed to her.

Earhart and Noonan crashed and were arrested by the Japanese. Japan would have made sure the fliers survived. They were valuable hostages. They could be traded for captured Japanese prisoners. They were released after the war in exchange for not trying the Japanese emperor for war crimes.

The findings of Operation Earhart were right. Native reports of the execution of Noonan and the death of Earhart were only rumors that had become popular tales. Officials secretly wanted to hide Earhart and Noonan in the United States.

CLOSING THE CASE FILE

▲▲▲▲▲▲▲▲▲▲▲▲▲▲▲▲▲▲▲▲▲▲▲▲▲▲▲▲▲▲▲

Earhart's around-the-world flight was not completed. But she did accomplish a personal goal. Before she started the flight, she wrote to her husband to explain her reasons for it: "I am quite aware of the hazards. I want to do it—because I want to do it. Women must try to do things as men have tried. When they fail, their failure must be but a challenge to others."

Earlier she had expressed her feelings about death to her friends by saying, "I'd like to go in my plane. Quickly."

Ten years before she vanished, Earhart was unknown. She worked at Denison House and flew when she could. A line from a poem she wrote then nicely sums up her life: "Each time we make a choice, we pay with courage . . . and count it fair."

Whatever happened to Earhart on her final flight, she would have counted it fair. A hero does not fear death.

But the world mourns a hero's death. That is probably why so many people continue to ask, What happened to Amelia Earhart?

CHRONOLOGY

▲▲▲▲▲▲▲▲▲▲▲▲▲▲▲▲▲▲▲▲▲▲▲▲▲▲▲▲▲▲▲▲

1897   July 24, Amelia Earhart is born.

1928   June 17–18, Lady Lindy flies the Atlantic.

1932   May 20–21, AE flies the Atlantic.

1937   March 17, Earhart and Noonan leave Oakland, California, to fly around the world from east to west.
March 20, The Electra is damaged in Hawaii.
June 1, Earhart and Noonan leave Miami, Florida, to fly around the world from west to east.
July 2, Earhart and Noonan vanish.
July 19, Official search is called off.

1941   December 8, U.S. declares war on Japan.

1945   August 15, V-J Day (Japan surrenders).

1966   Fred Goerner's *The Search for Amelia Earhart* is published.

1970	Joe Klaas's *Amelia Earhart Lives* is published.
1985	Vincent Loomis's *Amelia Earhart: The Final Story* is published.
1987	Thomas E. Devine's *Eyewitness: The Amelia Earhart Incident* is published.

RESOURCES

▲▲▲▲▲▲▲▲▲▲▲▲▲▲▲▲▲▲▲▲▲▲▲▲▲▲▲▲▲▲▲▲▲▲▲

SOURCES

Brian, Paul L., Jr. *Daughter of the Sky, The Story of Amelia Earhart.* New York: Duell, Sloan and Pearce, 1960.

Earhart, Amelia. *The Fun of It.* New York 1932. Reprint. Chicago: Academy Press, 1984.

Heinrichs, Waldo. *Threshold of War: Franklin D. Roosevelt and American Entry into World War II.* New York: Oxford University Press, 1988.

Moolman, Valerie. *Women Aloft.* Alexandria, Va.: Time-Life Books, 1981.

FURTHER READING FOR YOUNG READERS

Lauber, Patricia. *Lost Star.* New York: Scholastic, 1988.

Leder, Jane. *Amelia Earhart.* San Diego: Greenhaven Press, 1989.

INDEX

▲▲▲▲▲▲▲▲▲▲▲▲▲▲▲▲▲▲▲▲▲▲▲▲▲▲▲▲▲▲▲▲▲▲▲▲

J
B
EARHART

Larsen, Anita
   Amelia Earhart: Missing,
      Declared Dead